Full Impact

Suzanne Weyn

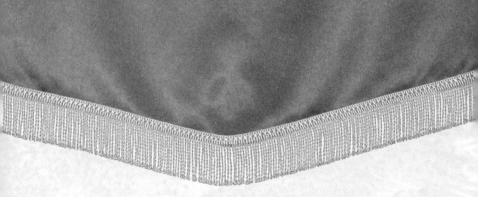

SURVIVING SOUTHSIDE

Full Impact

Suzanne Weyn

darbycreek

MINNEAPOLIS

Darby Creek
A division of Lerner Publishing Group, Inc.
241 First Avenue North
Minneapolis, MN 55401 U.S.A.

Website address: www.lernerbooks.com

The images in this book are used with the permission of: © Thomas Barwick/Digital Vision/Getty Images, (main image) front cover; © iStockphoto.com/Jill Fromer, (banner background) front cover and throughout interior; © iStockphoto.com/Naphtalina, (brick wall background) front cover and throughout interior.

Main body text set in Janson Text LT Std 55 Roman 12/17.5.
Typeface provided by Adobe Systems.

Library of Congress Cataloging-in-Publication Data

Weyn, Suzanne.
    Full impact / by Suzanne Weyn.
        p.   cm. — (Surviving Southside)
    ISBN 978-1-4677-0311-6 (lib. bdg. : alk. paper)
    [1. Football—Fiction. 2. High schools—Fiction. 3. Schools—Fiction.] I. Title.
PZ7.W539Ful 2013
[Fic]—dc23   2012029523

Manufactured in the United States of America
1 – BP – 12/31/12

This book is dedicated to Mrs. Laura O'Grady, head of the Hudson Valley Hospital Emergency Room, who took such good care of me when I got hit on the head. Many thanks.
—S.W.

CHAPTER 1

With the score tied and just minutes left on the clock, the Titans began running the ball downfield with a series of laterals.

Fullback Arnie Johnson sprinted toward the end zone. Halfback Norval Lamb saw two Cougar tackles gaining on Arnie and hoped Arnie saw them too.

Arnie pivoted when he noticed the Cougar players within a few feet of him, shifting from foot to foot in a lightning-quick dance.

Will Arnie take the ball out of bounds? Norval wondered. *Does he have enough time? Or will he get rid of it?*

As the Cougars pounced, Arnie released the football. It spiraled toward Norval. Without time to think, Norval leaped into the air, stretching to reach the ball.

He had it!

Ducking and zigzagging through the last line of Cougars, Norval had only one goal—to make it to the end zone.

The Titan fans in the bleachers roared with excitement as Norval pulled off a forward roll and scored the winning touchdown for Southside High.

Grinning widely, Norval pulled off his helmet. He danced a quick salsa step to show his delight. He knew the coaches would frown on too much gloating, but he couldn't resist. It had been a tight game from the start—this win hadn't come easily.

The Southside crowd continued cheering as Norval and his teammates jogged off the field. Arnie came alongside Norval and landed a friendly slap on Norval's back. "Good play, man!"

"Thanks. You too."

"Nah. It was all you. It was a gamble, but I knew you'd make it."

"Those tackles took you down hard," Norval said. "You okay?"

"Dude, please," Arnie replied, rubbing the back of his neck. "They knock me down, but I bounce back up."

When they reached the sidelines, their teammates gave them cheers, thumps, and hugs. The Southside cheerleaders sang a victory chant, leaping in the air and shaking their pom-poms.

A girl with silky black hair and large dark eyes wrapped Arnie in a hug. "You were amazing, Arnie!" Lara Velez cried.

Norval and Arnie exchanged smiling glances. Norval knew Arnie liked Lara, even though the guys all agreed she was a big flirt. "Thanks, Lara," Arnie said. "But Norval's the man today."

"Norval made the TD, but you're the one who carried the ball most of the way," Lara said.

"That's the truth!" Norval agreed. He raised his arm and high-fived Arnie.

Norval looked around and found his girlfriend, Sadie Collins, chatting with some of the other cheerleaders. He wanted to be sure she didn't think he was the one flirting with Lara. They had a good thing going—Norval didn't want to mess it up.

Sadie wasn't paying attention, though. Then—almost as if she could feel his eyes on her—she turned toward him and smiled.

Norval smiled back and waved.

"You and Sadie are still going strong, I see," Lara said.

"A month last week," Norval confirmed.

"You two make a cute couple," Lara said. "Poor Sadie. She didn't have a boyfriend for so long. Boys just didn't seem to notice her."

Norval rolled his eyes. The remark was pure Lara. "Well, she has one now."

"I'm happy for you guys," Lara said and then turned her attention to Arnie. "See you at Kadeem's for pizza. You're going, aren't you, Arnie?"

"I'll be there," Arnie said.

"Cool. I'll see you later, then," Lara said,

flashing him her most flirtatious smile as she danced away.

"Look out, man. Lara's coming for you. She's got you in her sights," Norval teased.

"I wouldn't mind," Arnie said, his eyes still on Lara.

Kadeem Jones, Southside's quarterback, stepped between Norval and Arnie and threw his arms over their shoulders. "Way to go!" he shouted. "My place for victory pizza!"

"We heard," Norval said. "We're in."

Kadeem jerked his head toward the stands, indicating the cluster of middle-aged men still lingering in the bleachers. "Scouts."

Norval recognized a few of them: one scout from Miller College, another from State University, and another scout from nearby Wendell College.

"You guys heard anything yet?" Kadeem asked.

Norval shook his head. Kadeem had already been recruited to play college ball for the Peterson Pirates. "Nothing yet for me," Arnie admitted. "Something better come through. A scholarship is the only way I'm going to college."

CHAPTER 2

N orval squeezed his legs together to balance the paper plate holding his pizza. Kadeem's parents had put out a great spread for the team. Norval couldn't imagine how much the tower of pizzas on the table must have cost them. But they'd been right to order so much. This team could *eat*! Especially after a game like the one they had just played.

Finishing his last bite of gyro pizza, Norval got up and headed back to the table for more. Lara was there with Maritza Rubio, another cheerleader. "Arnie was great today, wasn't he?" Norval said.

"I guess so. Whatever . . ." Lara grumbled. What had caused her enthusiasm to fade?

"What's going on?" Norval asked as he peeled another slice from the pie.

"I don't know. Go ask your buddy. When I tried to talk to him he just brushed me off."

"He's acting weird," Maritza added.

When Norval went to find Arnie, someone said he'd just left.

That's odd, Norval thought. Arnie hadn't even said goodbye. It wasn't like him.

He went and found Sadie. "Arnie just left all the sudden. Do you mind if I go try and find him? I'll be back in time to walk you home."

"Sure, go ahead," Sadie agreed. "Don't worry about me. Paige's mom is driving her home. I can get a ride with them."

Norval kissed her lightly. "Thanks. You're the best."

Norval left the apartment and caught up with Arnie in the building's main lobby.

"Leaving so soon? What's up?" he asked.

"I don't know," Arnie said with a shrug. "All the noise in there was getting on my nerves. Giving me a headache."

"Well, you managed to make Lara pretty mad. What went down?"

"Nothing, really. I just wasn't in the mood for her chatter. I guess she could tell." Arnie pushed the front door open and headed down the sidewalk.

Norval fell into step beside him. "I thought you liked Lara."

"I do. I think I'm just tired. And, like I said, I have this headache."

"Maybe you should text her later," Norval suggested. "She's obviously into you. At least, she was before you blew her off."

"I didn't blow her off. She's cute, man, but she's trouble. Look how she's making a big deal over nothing. We're not even together yet."

"She's a drama queen, sure," Norval said. "But I thought you had a thing for her."

"I did. I do," Arnie said.

"Is something else bugging you?" Norval asked.

"Maybe this scholarship thing is weighing on me. How come nobody came up to us today?"

"I don't know. But I didn't see them approach anyone."

"It's like I said—no athletic scholarship, no college."

"What about Southside CC?" Norval asked. "Could you swing that?"

"Community college?" Arnie cried. "They don't even have a football team! I'm not getting to the pros that way."

"I didn't know you were thinking pro ball."

Arnie reeled around, glaring. "What? Think I don't have what it takes?"

"Whoa, man!" Norval raised two hands to back Arnie up. "Don't take it like that. I just didn't know you had that in mind. I'm not sure I want to play pro. I haven't thought that far ahead. Right now I'm just hoping for a free ride through school to play some college ball."

"Not me. Ever since I played peewee touch football, going pro's all I've ever wanted."

Norval remembered Arnie as a little kid in their peewee football days. Arnie would complain that it was touch football and not tackle. He couldn't wait to really mix it up with the other team. And that's exactly what he did once they got to middle school.

No one was more fearless than Arnie. Some of the kids took to calling him Bouncing Arnie Johnson because he seemed to bounce back after every tackle. It wasn't surprising that Arnie wanted to play pro ball, once Norval thought about it. Football was what he lived for.

"Sorry for yelling at you, man," Arnie said, walking again. "I've just been cranky ever since the game ended."

"You seemed okay right after it," Norval pointed out. "Did something happen?"

"It's my head. It started pounding once I got to the party."

"Should you get it checked out?" Norval asked.

"It'll stop. The same thing happened after the last game. But it went away in a couple of hours."

They came to Arnie's apartment building, which was just a few buildings down from Norval's place. With a quick fist bump, Arnie headed up the front steps. "Later," he said as he pulled open the front door.

"Take something for your head. Get some sleep," Norval said from the sidewalk. "Call Lara."

"Sure, sure," Arnie replied. Flashing Norval a grin, he went inside.

As Norval walked toward his family's own apartment, he put Arnie out of his mind. A headache could make anyone cranky.

CHAPTER 3

The Titans' next big game was two weeks later, against Northside High. Norval joined his teammates at the thirty-yard line and got ready for kickoff.

Arnie looked distracted, like he was searching the bleachers. Following Arnie's gaze, Norval noticed scouts in the stands. He recognized the scouts from Wendell College and State U again. Then he spotted two more. One was from Croft College and the other from Phillips University.

Arnie turned to Norval and jerked his head toward the scouts. Norval nodded, then started trying to block the scouts from his mind. He needed to focus on the game. Hopefully Arnie would do the same.

Kadeem got into position and began calling plays. When he received the snap from the center, he quickly handed the ball off to Norval.

Norval raced forward for five yards while Arnie ran interference against the Northside defensive end. With his head down, Norval barreled his way for another yard, confident that Arnie would block the defender. In the next second, though, Norval noticed two more Northside players coming at him from a different direction. Too fast—he couldn't outrun them. He had to get rid of the ball.

Is Arnie open, or is that defensive end still on him? Norval wondered.

No. Arnie was clear! The defensive end was heading toward Norval.

Pivoting, Norval lateralled the ball to Arnie. Before Arnie could catch it, the

Northside defensive end turned back and slammed into him. The two players who'd been threatening Norval also changed course and piled onto Arnie.

The whistle blew.

Norval watched as the Northside defense got to their feet. Arnie lay on the ground, still.

Assistant Coach Green hurried out onto the field and knelt beside Arnie. Norval was relieved to see Arnie get up onto his elbows. At least he was conscious.

Head Coach Gannon called for a time-out as the medics came onto the field. Arnie lifted up his helmet to speak to them.

Even though Norval couldn't hear what was being said, he had the feeling that Arnie was telling them he was okay. To prove the point, Arnie rose to his feet—then staggered back.

Coach Green steadied him. After more talk, the medics left the field and Arnie walked slowly off to the sideline with the two coaches on either side of him.

CHAPTER 4

Norval joined his other teammates as they crowded around Arnie on the bench. "I'm good. Really!" Arnie said. "My helmet got creamed, but I'm okay."

Arnie smiled and pointed to a crack that ran all the way up the side of the helmet. "*That* could've been my head!" He twirled it on his hand. "Anybody have a spare? This one isn't going to do me much good for the rest of the game."

"Forget it, Arnie," Coach Green told him. "You're sitting the rest of this game out."

Arnie leaped to his feet, protesting. "Come on, Coach! I want to play. I told you, I'm perfectly fine!"

"Maybe I'll put you in for fourth quarter," Coach Green said. "Rest up for now, and we'll see how you're doing by then."

"Aw, come on!" Arnie said. "I'm good to play now. Honest!"

Norval knew Arnie was thinking of the scouts in the stands.

"No way, Johnson," Coach Gannon said. "Calm down, or you're benched for longer than this game."

"You can't do this to me, Coach!" Arnie cried.

Coach Green shot Arnie a warning look. "Last time I'm saying it. Sit down."

Arnie muttered something under his breath as he slumped back onto the bench.

Arnie is really pushing his luck with all that arguing, Norval thought. Fortunately, the coaches didn't seem to have heard him.

"Don't sweat it, Arnie," Norval said. "The

scouts will be back. It doesn't reflect on you. Even the pros get pulled out when they're injured."

"Yeah, well, they already have contracts," Arnie grumbled.

"Come on, man. The scouts know how it is."

"Yeah? How is it? They see me get pulled and they say, 'This guy can't take a hit. He doesn't have the stuff.'"

"It's not like that," Norval said.

The rest of the game was close. This time, though, there was no thrilling final touchdown. The Titans lost.

After the game, Norval met back up with Arnie, who was talking to Lara and Maritza by the bleachers. "How you feelin'?" he asked.

"Completely fine," Arnie said. "Wonderful! Not a scratch on me."

"And your head? Any headache this time?"

Arnie tapped his head. "I'm having some trouble telling the voices apart."

"What?" Norval asked.

"I'm playing with you, man," Arnie confessed with a laugh. "I'm totally okay.

Coach was crazy to pull me out of that game. I was so down to play."

"It was really dumb," Lara added. "If Green had played him, you guys would have won for sure."

"I don't know about that," Arnie said, trying to sound modest.

Norval was glad to see that Arnie had straightened things out with Lara. "Maybe so," he said. "Still, it's better to be safe."

Arnie scoffed. "It's better to win!"

"I don't know about that," Norval said.

"What? You think we didn't win 'cause I let the team down?" Arnie snapped.

"I never said that!" Norval said.

"Sounded like it," Arnie mumbled.

"No way." Norval slapped Arnie's back. "Anyways, I'm glad you're okay."

As Norval spoke, he thought he saw Arnie wince. "You really okay?" he asked.

"Don't be such an old lady," Arnie said, smiling once more. "I told you. I'm great."

CHAPTER 5

Norval was standing at his locker the next day when he saw Coach Green coming toward him. "Would you come see me in my office sometime today, Norval?" Coach asked.

"Sure. I have a study hall third period," Norval replied, growing worried.

"Don't look so nervous," Coach Green said with a smile. "I just want to talk to you about something. Not a big deal."

"Okay. I'll see you later."

Despite the reassurance from Coach Green, Norval couldn't stop wondering what the meeting would be about. Southside had lost its last game. Maybe Coach felt Norval hadn't played his best. Would he want Norval to put in extra practice time? Could one of his teachers have complained about his grades? He hadn't done well on his last chemistry test. But they wouldn't pull him from the team for that, right?

On the way to the coach's office he passed Arnie in the hall. "Do you have any idea why Coach Green would want to talk to me today?" Norval asked.

"Maybe one of the college scouts contacted him about you," Arnie said. "It's possible."

"That would be cool," Norval said, but he wasn't convinced. Even though Coach Green's tone had been casual, Norval sensed that the coach was concerned about something.

Leaving Arnie, Norval continued on toward the coach's office.

"Hey, man." Kadeem thumped Norval's shoulder as they passed in the hall. Norval grabbed Kadeem's arm.

"Hey, Coach Green just said he wanted to talk to me about something. Like, in his office. You have any idea why?"

"I don't know, but he asked to see me, too," Kadeem said.

"Are you worried?" Norval asked.

Kadeem shrugged. "Not yet. I'll wait 'til I hear what he has to say."

Kadeem was right, Noval thought. Why worry until he had something to worry about? With a nod, he left Kadeem and kept walking over to the athletic department.

Coach Green greeted him when Norval got to the office. "Have a seat, Norval."

"Coach, I can put in the extra practice time if you want, but I can't do that and do the extra chemistry on top of it," Norval said before the coach could say anything. "There's just not enough time to—"

"Hold on, Norval," Coach Green stopped him. "It's not you I'm concerned about."

Relief flooded Norval. "It's not?"

"No. It's Arnie. You know him pretty well, don't you? Have you noticed anything unusual about him lately?"

Norval felt he needed to be careful how he answered. He didn't want to say anything that would get Arnie in trouble. "What kind of unusual?" he asked the coach.

"Lack of focus?" Coach Green said. "Maybe fatigue, headache."

Norval ran through a mental list. Arnie had complained of headaches. And he definitely had not been himself at Kadeem's get-together. He remembered, too, how Arnie had snapped at him after the game yesterday.

"Arnie isn't drinking or drugging, if that's what you're asking," Norval said.

"It's not that," Coach Green said. "I'm worried that Arnie has gotten hit in the head too often. I want to know if he's showing symptoms of a concussion."

CHAPTER 6

N orval tried to recall what he knew about the word *concussion*. The only thing that came to mind was that it was what everyone got upset about when someone had a head injury.

The year before, a player named Ty Hendrickson had been knocked unconscious on the field. Norval had visited the hospital along with Coach Gannon.

A doctor had put Ty's head in a machine to take a scan of his brain. Then the doctor had said that there was no bleeding in Ty's brain—he was good to go. By the next game, Ty was up and running again.

Ty no longer played running back because of some trouble he'd had with the police. It was too bad, since Ty had been a good player. Ty's trouble had worked out well for Arnie, though. He took up Ty's position afterward, which helped him stand out to the scouts.

"Did Ty Hendrickson have a concussion?" Norval asked. "I thought the doctor said he was all right."

"All he really said was that Ty had no internal bleeding. Sometimes the symptoms of a concussion show up right away. Other times it can take longer."

"What do Arnie's parents think?" Norval asked.

"I don't want to call and upset them until I have a better idea if there's anything to worry about," Coach Green said. "That's where you come in."

Norval didn't like the sound of that.

"Research is showing that concussions are

much more serious than anyone realized," Coach said. "If one player runs into another player at full speed—that's about the same as getting hit by a car going forty miles an hour. Especially at the college or pro level."

"It feels more like getting flattened by a truck," Norval said. He had been knocked down any number of times. He knew firsthand that it wasn't fun.

The coach nodded. "Researchers are looking at the brains of dead athletes and finding that they don't look the same as the brains of nonathletes of the same age. They think that concussion injuries can be a problem later in life, even if the concussion's from when the player was young."

"If it doesn't show up at first, how can you watch for it?"

"There are still signs to look for right away," Coach Green said. "The things I mentioned earlier—headache, fatigue, problems focusing. Vision problems, too. Unsteadiness, vomiting . . ."

"But Arnie has never been knocked out cold," Norval said.

"You don't have to be. Any tackle can be enough for your brain to get rocked."

"Isn't that why we wear helmets?"

"Helmets help prevent head fractures, not concussions. Your head still feels the impact. Since we started wearing better helmets, the number of fractures has gone down, but not the number of concussions. Some doctors even think concussions have gone up. They say good helmets make players want to play rougher."

"Have you talked to Arnie about this?" Norval asked.

"I did," Coach Green said. "He says he has no problems—he's just great."

"So why don't you believe him?"

"Players may not tell the truth. They don't want to be sidelined. Arnie's not playing like he used to. His timing's off. And he's gotten hit a lot this season. I want you to keep an eye on him. Let me know if he shows any of the signs we talked about. I'll take it from there."

"I don't know, Coach," Norval said. "That'd be kind of like spying on one of my friends."

"It's more like watching out for him," the coach said.

It still feels all wrong, Norval thought.

"Honestly, Coach, I'd rather not," Norval said, getting to his feet. "If Arnie found out I was doing this he'd be really mad. If he says he's fine, then he's fine."

"Think about it," Coach Green said as Norval stepped out of the office.

CHAPTER 7

"What's on your mind, Norval?" Sadie asked as they left the movie theater later that night.

"Nothing," he answered.

"Oh, yeah?" she challenged. "How did the movie end?"

"Everything blew up."

"That's right. And it was sad that they all died, wasn't it?"

"Very sad," Norval agreed.

Sadie thumped his arm. "They escaped!"

"They did?" Norval felt genuinely surprised. He really had lost track of the plot—his mind kept wandering back to the conversation with Coach Green.

"Tell me what's going on," Sadie said.

"Okay," Norval agreed with a sigh.

━━ ━━ ━━ ━━ ━━

"So, are you going to do what your coach asked?"

"No," Norval said. "I told him I didn't want to."

"Did Coach Green get mad at you?" Sadie asked.

"I'm the one who should be mad," Norval said, his voice rising. "It's not right for him to put me in that position. He's the one who should be watching Arnie, not me. He's the coach!"

"What about Arnie's parents?"

"That's another thing!" Norval cried. "Coach says he doesn't want to upset them. So he tries to lay it on me. It's like he didn't even think about whether *I'd* get upset . . ."

"Are you upset?" Sadie asked.

"Of course I am! How would you feel if the cheer coach asked you to spy on Paige?"

"I don't know," Sadie said. "Weird, I guess."

"Right? She's your friend. Don't you tell her everything? You don't keep secrets from her."

"That's true. Have you told Arnie about this?"

Norval let out a sigh. "Not yet."

"Why not?"

Once they reached Sadie's apartment building, Norval took a seat on the steps. Sadie settled in beside him. "If I tell him, then he'll hide any symptoms he's experiencing. He won't even talk to me about it."

"I thought you refused to watch him," Sadie said.

"I refused to spy for Coach Green. I still want to keep an eye on him, though. What if he does have a concussion? Arnie's stubborn. He wants to be recruited so badly. He'd play even if his foot was falling off."

"What will you do if you think he has the symptoms?"

"I'll talk to Arnie on the side. I won't blow the whistle on him, though. What kind of friend would I be if I did that?"

Sadie nodded. "How serious do you think this concussion stuff is?"

"I don't know. Coach made it sound like it was the end of the world or something. But I can't believe it's that serious. Guys get their clocks cleaned all the time."

"Well, you'll just have to keep an eye on Arnie," Sadie said.

"I know. Hey, look, I gotta go. Thanks for listening," Norval said, and kissed Sadie goodnight.

CHAPTER 8

All that night Norval stared at his bedroom ceiling. Arnie said he was all right. Why should Norval doubt him? Besides, it was none of Norval's business.

Coach Green should never have asked him to watch Arnie. And yet, Arnie was awake at 2:00 A.M., losing sleep over it, even though he had a chemistry quiz in the morning. He hadn't even been able to study because he couldn't concentrate. Didn't Coach know anything about friendship? A guy didn't spy on his friend. It was just wrong. If Coach Green asked how Arnie seemed, Norval would say, "Perfectly fine!"

Norval pulled a blanket over his shoulder and turned on his side. His mind was made up.

━ ━ ━ ━ ━

When Norval got to school the next morning, he saw Arnie heading toward class. He hurried to catch up with him.

"Hey, man, how's it going?"

"Not bad," Arnie replied. "What did Coach want yesterday?"

"Ah, nothing."

Arnie raised an eyebrow. "Nothing?"

"Nothing much." Norval tried to seem casual, but his mind was racing. Should he tell Arnie that the coach was concerned about him? That he'd asked for Norval's help?

When he spoke, only a half-truth came out. "He asked if I had noticed any of the guys on the team acting strange."

"Strange how?"

"Like, if any of them have taken too many hits to the head." He went on to tell Arnie about the symptoms he had been told to look for.

"Have you noticed anybody like that?" Arnie asked.

"No," Norval replied. "Have you?"

"Nope."

They continued on to English 12 together. "Today's our test on *Gilgamesh*," their teacher, Mr. Wilson, reminded them. "As long as you finished the reading, this shouldn't be hard. Take out a sheet of paper, everybody."

Mr. Wilson pointed to three questions on the whiteboard. The class got busy answering them.

As the teacher had promised, the questions weren't difficult. Even though chemistry was a challenge, English was always a breeze for Norval. And he'd enjoyed the action in *Gilgamesh*. The ancient style of writing wasn't always easy to read, but at least it had fight scenes.

When Norval finished, he put down his pen and looked up. About half the class had already completed the test. They sat waiting for the other half to be done. Arnie gazed out the window. Norval was glad to see that he wasn't still struggling to finish. He was fine. Focused.

At the end of class, Mr. Wilson collected the tests and dismissed the class. Norval waited for Arnie by the door. They were about to leave when Mr. Wilson called to Arnie. He held up one of the test sheets. "Mr. Johnson, what happened?"

The paper had Arnie's name written on the top line—and that was all!

"Didn't you read the book?" Mr. Wilson asked.

"Most of it," Arnie answered.

"Then why didn't you write anything?"

"The questions didn't make sense to me," Arnie said with a feeble smile.

Mr. Wilson ruffled through the other papers. "They seemed to make sense to everyone else."

Arnie shrugged.

"Mr. Johnson, go home and finish the book. Then come see me about a possible retest. You have until Friday."

"Thanks," Arnie said.

Arnie and Norval headed out into the hall together. "Didn't read the book, huh?" Norval assumed. "I thought you said you liked it."

"I did—at first. I got through three-quarters of it. I lost interest after that, though."

"You could have answered the first two questions, at least," Norval said.

"Maybe. But for real—I couldn't make sense of those questions."

"They weren't exactly hard. Are you feeling all right?"

"Kind of tired."

Norval opened his mouth to ask another question, but Arnie cut him off. "It's nothing. I've been seeing more of Lara. We've been going out, you know—staying up late and all."

"That's cool," Norval said. Really, it was none of his business.

"You're right. It's cool," Arnie said. "Everything's cool."

"Good," Norval said.

His next class was trig. Arnie wasn't in it. Norval had to play close attention in math. Like chemistry, it didn't come easily to him.

So for the length of that class he didn't think of Arnie, or football, or anything else but trigonometry. In a way, the class was a pleasant distraction from his other worries.

On the way out, he met up with Kadeem, who was also in trig. "What did Coach want to talk to you about?" Kadeem asked.

Norval hesitated. Coach Green had spoken to him privately. He wasn't sure if it was right to reveal Arnie's business to another player, even if it was Kadeem.

Kadeem lowered his voice. "Was it about Arnie?"

"Yeah. Did he talk to you too?"

"Yeah," Kadeem said.

"Do you think there's anything wrong with him?" Norval asked.

"I don't know, but I haven't really been paying attention," Kadeem replied. "I'll watch him more closely from now on."

"Me too," Norval agreed. "But that doesn't mean I'm going to tell the coach what I think. I don't think it was right for him to ask us to do that."

Kadeem nodded. "I know what you mean. But it doesn't seem right not to do it, either. You know what I mean?"

Norval did know, but for some reason he didn't feel like admitting it. "Not really. Doesn't it feel like spying to you?" he asked as they walked down the hall.

"In a way," Kadeem said. "But I hope Arnie's as fine as he keeps saying he is."

"Look," Norval said. "If this is as big a deal as Coach Green makes it out to be, why doesn't he take charge of it? Let him watch Arnie."

"We're around Arnie way more than Coach Green is. I think he is watching Arnie. He probably just wants some backup."

"So you're going to be watching Arnie too?"

"Yeah."

That made Norval feel a lot better. With Coach Green and Kadeem on the case, they didn't really need him.

"But I'm not tight with him like you are," Kadeem added. "Arnie's a great guy, but we don't hang out. I don't even have any classes with him this year. You see him the most."

Norval nodded. At first he'd been happy that Kadeem was in this with him. But—if he really thought about it—talking to Kadeem would be the same as going to Coach Green. It would have the same result. Arnie could end up being sidelined—maybe for the rest of the season.

Then Norval remembered how Kadeem had talked about things. He tried not to worry until he was sure he had a reason to worry. And he wouldn't turn in Arnie unless there was a reason he was sure of. Norval decided he would try to do the same.

CHAPTER 9

The Titans had to win their next game in order to qualify for the semifinals. They were scheduled against the Hempstead Huskers.

"I heard they've been working on defense since the last time we played them," Kadeem said in the locker room before they went out.

"We'll run a strong interference," Jerome Stevens said confidently.

"We're going to have to really block them hard," Kadeem added.

"We can contain them," Arnie said. "This game is in the bag."

Norval wasn't so sure. Southside High was pretty evenly matched with Hempstead, especially if the Huskers had strengthened their defensive line.

Coach Green came into the locker room. "Arnie, Norval, Jerome. I need a word with you." They huddled around the coach in a corner away from the other players. "I just talked to those scouts from Miller College. They were asking me about the three of you."

"Me? Are you sure?" Arnie asked eagerly.

Coach smiled. "Yeah, you, Arnie."

Arnie grinned.

"Stay sharp out there today. My feeling is they might make one or all of you an offer, depending on what they see in this game," Coach Green continued.

"Awesome!" Arnie said.

Out on the field, Norval located the scouts in the stands. Then, once again, he tried to put them out of his head. Thinking about scouts during the game would just throw him off.

Midway through the first quarter, a Husker was about to sack Kadeem when he lateralled the ball to Norval. Norval leaped for it, but two other Huskers took him down.

Arnie swept up the ball before it hit the ground. Head down, he barreled forward, a straight shot at the end zone in front of him. The Southside fans went wild in the stands.

Arnie lifted up his head and looked into the cheering crowd, slowing down slightly before he reached the goal line. Without realizing it, he veered into the path of two defenders.

No! Norval thought, cringing as the two Huskers tackled Arnie to the ground.

— — — — —

Throughout the rest of the first half, Arnie and Norval were tackled repeatedly. Kadeem had been right. The Huskers were more formidable than they'd been the last time the Titans played them.

With minutes to go at the end of the second quarter, Kadeem threw a short pass to

Arnie, who snagged the ball over the head of the defender. A couple of teammates blocked some of the Huskers as they came after him. Several more defenders broke through.

As the Huskers gained on Arnie, Norval tried to get into position, should Arnie decide to lateral the ball.

Arnie juked left and right as he muscled toward the end zone. *He's showing off for the scouts*, Norval realized.

With only a couple of yards to go, Arnie was dragging two defenders along with him. Then a third Husker hit Arnie hard. He went down at the one-yard line, losing the ball as he fell.

After the tackle, Arnie slowly pulled himself up. As the whistle blew to end the half, he slouched off the field, veering to the side as though he were off-balance.

Kadeem jogged alongside Norval, then tilted his helmet in Arnie's direction. "See that?"

Norval nodded. He was glad Kadeem had noticed. It proved to Norval that he hadn't been imagining it—Arnie had weaved to the right just then. It wasn't a good sign.

CHAPTER 10

In the locker room, Jerome confronted Arnie. "What's the matter with you, man? I was open. Norval was clear. Why didn't you get rid of the ball? You could see those guys were coming for you."

Arnie took off his helmet and stared at him blankly. He didn't even seem angry. Just confused. "I didn't see them."

"How could you not?" Jerome shouted. "They were hanging on you!"

The other players began to gather around. Arnie held his blank stare.

"Answer me!" Jerome demanded. "Are you high? I think you're stoned."

Norval stepped in. "Come on, Jerome. You know that's not true. Tell him, Arnie."

"No, I'm not stoned," Arnie said flatly.

"You're a liar," Jerome shouted, shoving Arnie.

Arnie staggered back and tripped over the bench. A sickening crack sounded as Arnie's head hit the cement floor. Arnie's eyes shut. His face seemed to relax—go limp, almost.

Norval knelt beside him. "Arnie! Arnie!" he cried, trying to rouse his friend. He was rising to get help when Arnie's eyes flickered open.

"How do you feel?" Norval asked urgently.

Arnie looked at him but didn't answer.

Kadeem peered at Arnie from over Norval's shoulder. "What's going on, Arnie?"

Arnie pulled himself up.

"I didn't mean for you to hit your head like that," Jerome said sullenly. "I'm sorry, man."

Arnie sat on the bench and dismissed Jerome with a wave. "Whatever." He looked to

Kadeem and Norval. "I'm not stoned. I would never do that, especially not during a game."

"We know. It's cool," Norval said.

"You okay to play the rest of the game?" Kadeem asked.

"Yeah. Definitely."

Kadeem gave Arnie's shoulder a friendly slap and walked off. Norval sat beside Arnie. "Looked like you were somewhere else for a couple of seconds. Are you sure you should play?"

"What are you? My mom?" Arnie said, getting up. "Of course I can play. There are scouts out there."

Arnie's timing was off in the second half and so was his judgment, but the Titans won the game. They still had a shot at the play-offs.

"Sorry I was so awful today," Arnie murmured as the team left the locker room together.

"You probably shouldn't have played after getting that crack on the head during halftime," Norval replied. "Go home. Get some sleep."

"Yeah. That's what I need. I'll be better in the morning."

CHAPTER 11

Arnie didn't come to school on Monday.
Norval tried his cell, but Arnie didn't pick
up. He didn't respond to Norval's texts, either.

Arnie and Norval had different schedules
on Tuesday, so Norval didn't see him then,
either. But he assumed that Arnie would at
least be at practice. To Norval's surprise,
Arnie wasn't.

Arnie would have to be really sick to miss practice,
Norval thought. *Maybe something's seriously wrong.*

"I'm worried about Arnie," Kadeem said as he and Norval headed off the field. "He's never missed drills before."

"I know," Norval agreed. "And he got hit bad on Saturday—twice on the field and once in the locker room."

"Yeah," Kadeem recalled. "That's a lot of damage in one day."

"Did you tell Coach about what happened in the locker room?" Norval asked.

Kadeem shook his head. "I didn't want him to take Arnie out of the game. He got up right away. Did you tell?"

"No," Norval said. "Same reason."

"Want me to check on him?"

"I'll do it," Norval said. "I pass his place on my way home."

"Great. Let me know what's going on," Kadeem said as he jogged toward the locker room.

"Hey, Norval!"

Lara Velez approached him before he entered the locker room. "You looked great out there today."

"Thanks."

"I hear you have colleges looking to make you offers," Lara went on. "You'll definitely get in. You were awesome last game."

"Thanks, Lara."

"I think maybe you and I should get together and hang out some night, Norval," Lara said. "What do you think?"

She smiled at him, her dark eyes sparkling. What was going on? Why was she coming on so strong?

"I don't think Arnie would like that too much," Norval replied. "Aren't the two of you kind of together?"

"Not anymore," Lara said firmly.

"What happened?" Norval asked.

"I was supposed to go to the movies with him on Saturday night after the game. He just left me hanging. He called later that night and said he fell asleep. I let it go. But then he was supposed to come over last night, too, and he never showed—again."

New worries hit Norval. "Did you talk to him?"

"No! He totally blew me off—wouldn't even return my texts," Lara said.

"So you thought you'd get back at him by hitting on one of his best friends. You know Sadie and I are together."

"Oh sure," Lara snarled. "Like you're such a great guy that you'd never cheat."

"I don't think I'm such a great guy, but I do know that Sadie and I are solid. She wouldn't mess around with someone else, and I wouldn't do it to her."

"Forget you, Norval!" Lara said. "I was just being friendly. Don't flatter yourself."

Norval shook his head as Lara stormed away, then headed into the locker room. *Arnie would be better off without Lara*, he thought. It made him appreciate Sadie that much more. He felt lucky that they were together.

CHAPTER 12

Inside the locker room, Norval asked the other players if they had heard from Arnie. None of them had. It wasn't like Arnie not to text or call.

Norval was about to leave the mostly empty locker room when Coach Green tapped him on the shoulder. "I noticed Arnie wasn't here today," he said. "Anything you want to tell me?"

"Nothing I could really say for sure," Norval replied.

"He took some bad hits last game," Coach

Green reminded him. "And Jerome told me about the scuffle in the locker room. I think he was worried someone else would tell me first."

The coach fixed his hard, meaningful stare on Norval.

"What?" Norval asked, his resentment rising. Why was watching Arnie his job? "Do you mean I should have told you?"

"He got clocked *again*, Norval," Coach Green said, frowning. "Didn't you think I should know that after everything we talked about?"

Norval didn't want to be sanctioned for disrespect, so he tried to control himself. "I told you I wouldn't spy on Arnie. Don't you remember?"

"He lost consciousness," Coach Green said. He seemed to be fighting his own temper. "Someone should have told me sooner. I wouldn't have let him play the rest of the game if I'd known."

"He was only out for a second."

"A person doesn't need to lose consciousness to suffer a concussion. The fact that he actually passed out makes things that much more serious, though. I called his house to speak to his parents, but they weren't in. I left a message. So far they haven't returned my call. You or Kadeem should have told me what happened. Why can't you guys get that through your heads?"

"It just seems wrong," Norval said. "We're teammates!"

"That's exactly why you guys should be looking out for one another!" Coach Green cried.

"I'll stop over there on my way home," Norval said.

"Great," the coach said, his voice calm again. "Please talk to me when you find out how he's doing. At the very least, promise me you'll talk sense to Arnie if you think he's got problems related to a concussion."

Without waiting for Norval's reply, Coach Green walked out.

Norval snapped up his jacket. The coach's anxiety might have been contagious. What if something bad had happened to Arnie because Norval didn't want the responsibility of reporting on him? He needed to assure himself that Arnie really was all right.

CHAPTER 13

When Norval buzzed Arnie's apartment, no one answered. Norval went back to the sidewalk and called up to the second-floor window.

"Hey, Arnie!"

A few minutes later, Arnie came to the window. When he saw it was Norval, he buzzed him in.

"What's up, Arnie?" Norval asked as he stepped into Arnie's small apartment.

"Did you knock before? I was asleep—sorry if I didn't hear you."

"Are you sick or something?"

"Kind of."

"I've been calling you. Texting, too," Norval said. "Why haven't you answered me?"

Arnie turned away from him. "I told you. I've been sleeping a lot. Just been tired lately."

"Too tired to pick up the phone?" Norval asked. "You want to tell me what's going on? Lara said you blew her off twice. She's steamed."

"Oh, the hell with her. She's such a pain."

"Well, how come you were blowing me off too?"

"I don't feel like talking to anybody."

"Because you're tired, right?" Norval asked. "And that's it?"

Arnie hesitated before answering. "Something's going on with my eyes, too," he admitted. "Things are kind of flickering, you know?"

"Weird. Does it hurt?" Norval asked.

Arnie closed his eyes. "No. But it's like everything's jumping."

As he spoke, Arnie put his hands to his midsection. The next moment, he sprinted to the bathroom down the hall.

Seconds later, retching sounds echoed from inside. Once it grew quiet inside, Norval knocked on the door. "You okay?"

The door opened, and Arnie reappeared, looking pale.

"Sit down," Norval said, turning on the kitchen faucet and filling a glass with water. "What's going on?" he asked, handing the glass to Arnie.

"I don't know. I keep puking."

"How long has that been happening?"

"A couple of weeks," Arnie said.

"Weeks? Have you been to a doctor?"

"Nope. I feel better once I throw up."

"Arnie, listen," Norval said. "Coach Green thinks you have a concussion. He asked me to keep an eye you and tell him what I see. He's worried about you."

Arnie leaped to his feet. "Did you tell him anything?"

"Hold on! I told him I wouldn't do it. But

now I'm thinking maybe I should."

"I don't believe you!" Arnie cried. "You've been ratting me out. How could you do this to me?"

"I wouldn't say anything to him without talking to you first," Norval said. "But I'm starting to agree with Coach. I think you've got a concussion, man."

CHAPTER 14

Arnie swore and slammed his hand on the kitchen table. "You're not a doctor!" he shouted. "Neither is Coach Green!"

"You have a lot of concussion symptoms," Norval said calmly. There was no sense getting as angry as Arnie. A shouting match was the last thing they needed.

"Like what?" Arnie asked.

"Like vomiting?"

"It's probably food poisoning," Arnie argued.

"Food poisoning doesn't last two weeks," Norval said. "Mood swings are another symptom."

"I've been okay."

"No you haven't, man," Norval said. "You've been mean as hell."

"That's just 'cause of the headaches."

"Headaches are another symptom." Norval thought back to Arnie's blank test paper and what Coach Green had said about lack of focus. "And you never explained why you stood Lara up twice. What was that about?"

"I forgot. She's making a big deal out of nothing. It just slipped my mind."

"Twice? You forgot twice?"

"So what? You're just like her—making a fuss over nothing."

Suddenly angry shouts reached them from down the hall. Behind a closed door, a man and woman were having an argument. Norval looked to Arnie with questioning eyes.

"It's just my parents," Arnie said. "They're always fighting."

Norval felt embarrassed for Arnie and

tried to ignore the rising voices. "You have to get yourself checked out by a doctor."

"No!" Arnie cried. "So what if I have a concussion? There's nothing to do but wait for it to heal. There's no medicine—it just has to get better. And it will."

"Not if you keep getting hit," Norval said.

The yelling from the other room got louder. Something crashed against a wall.

Arnie wilted down into one of the kitchen chairs. He cradled his head in his hands. "You can't tell Coach. It would screw me over big time. I can't stand living here. They fight all the time. I've got to get out, and the only way that will happen is if I get a football scholarship."

"Coach left them a phone message," Norval told him.

"I know. I got to it first and deleted it," Arnie said. "If the coach pulls me out for the rest of the season, there won't be any recruitment offers. No scholarship. I'm telling you, I'll go nuts if I have to spend any more time in this apartment."

"If you won't go to a doctor, I have to tell the coach," Norval said.

"I'm begging you, Norval. Don't do it. I can't take all the fighting. The only thing that keeps me going is the hope that I'll get to college."

No wonder Arnie was so desperate to get out, Norval thought. How could he ruin Arnie's chances?

"Norval, no kidding. Please," Arnie said. He seemed close to tears.

Norval wished he had never heard the word *concussion*. "Go to a doctor, Arnie. If you do, I won't say anything."

"All right. I'll go. I swear. Just don't talk to Coach or anyone else. Promise?"

"All right. I promise." Even as he said the words, though, Norval worried that he'd spoken too quickly. He hoped it wouldn't be a promise he'd regret keeping.

CHAPTER 15

N orval sat in front of his computer later that
night, browsing YouTube videos about
concussions. The news was bad—even worse
than he had thought. He listened to experts
who had studied the brains of athletes who
had died. A number of the athletes showed
signs of the problems that Coach Green had
mentioned. These athletes had died long after
their concussions, though. Concussions could
have much more immediate effects.

Norval stayed glued to the screen as he watched personal accounts from teen athletes who had been affected. Some of their symptoms were mild. Some were severe. Some of the kids had suffered so much brain damage that they couldn't finish school tests anymore, or even remember what they had learned. Some had tried to soothe the depression or rage they felt after their brain injuries by turning to drugs or alcohol. Some of them had to be placed in special classes at school because they could no longer keep up with the work.

Norval remembered the blank looks on Arnie's face during the English quiz and when Jerome had been accusing him of drug use. It was almost as if he hadn't understood what was being said to him.

With a worried sigh, Norval watched another video. This one was on something called secondary impact syndrome.

When the brain is healing itself from a concussion, the narrator said, *a second hit could cause a massive swelling in the brain. The secondary impact could be as slight as a mild knock to the head. It sets off a reaction even more severe than the brain's reaction to the original hard hit.*

Norval sat back in his chair, stunned.

A secondary impact concussion could cause death.

Arnie had been hit hard several times in the last few weeks alone. Who knew how many times he'd been hit before that?

Norval picked up his cell and called Arnie. "Arnie, do one thing for me," he said when Arnie picked up. "Go to BIAV.net." Norval had found the site after clicking around YouTube. It was the Brain Injury Association of Virginia's website. "Just read some of the stuff on there, okay? I think you really need to consider sitting out."

Arnie started to curse. "You just don't get it, do you, Norval? If you say anything about this to the coach, you and me are going to have a big problem."

"Don't be that way, Arnie," Norval said. "Come on. Be smart. We've been friends for years—you've got to trust me on this."

"Why should I, Norval? You've always been jealous of me."

"J-j-jealous?" Norval sputtered. "Are you crazy?"

"You heard me," Arnie said. "Jealous." Without another word, he hung up the phone.

Norval sat there, stunned. Arnie really was losing it.

He felt angry, devastated. Arnie's words had hurt him. And staying angry would be easier than staying hurt. Norval was done with Arnie, he decided. From that moment on, he didn't care what happened to Arnie Johnson.

CHAPTER 16

A rnie was back in school the next day, but he kept away from Norval until they passed each other in the hall before practice.

Norval tried to ignore Arnie, but Arnie grabbed his arm. "Back off, man," Norval growled.

"Hey, listen to me Norval," Arnie said. "I've got to talk to you."

Norval stopped to face him. "Make it fast."

"I don't blame you for being mad, okay?

I've been acting like a jerk to everybody lately. I don't know what's wrong with me. I'm sorry about last night."

"It doesn't matter," Norval said.

"No. I feel bad. Really. You're making too big a deal out of this concussion thing, though. I don't want to be benched. There are only a few weeks left of the season. I'll get better after that."

Norval looked at Arnie. The guy seemed really sincere and . . . scared. Norval couldn't hold on to his anger when his friend looked so wrung out.

"I haven't said anything to Coach Green. And I won't. Why don't you say you're sick? Stay out of school for a while so you can get better," Norval suggested.

"What am I going to say is wrong with me?"

"Say you have the flu. You're throwing up, aren't you?"

Arnie looked at the floor, as if considering Norval's words. But when he turned back to Norval, his face was twisted with anger. "You'd like that, huh?" Arnie snarled.

"What are you talking about?" Norval asked.

"You'd look pretty good to the Miller College scouts without me in the way. You could get with Lara."

"That's crazy. I don't even like Lara," Norval said. "I'm with Sadie."

"That's not what Lara told me. She said you were hitting on her."

"She was trying to make you jealous because you stood her up. She's probably mad that I blew her off. And anyway, we're friends. I'm not going to go after someone you're seeing," Norval said. "Plus, I wouldn't do that to Sadie."

"We're not friends," Arnie yelled. "If you were my friend you wouldn't be trying to get me kicked off the team."

"That's nuts, Arnie. You're losing it," Norval said.

"I'm about to," Arnie growled, and shoved Norval.

Coach Green came up and got between them. "What's the trouble here?"

Norval drew a deep breath. This was the moment. It was time to admit that he thought Coach was right—Arnie was suffering a number of concussion symptoms.

"I asked what the problem was," Coach Green said.

"It's about a girl," Norval told him. "He thinks I'm interested in his girlfriend, but I'm not."

"Do you believe him?" the coach asked Arnie.

"I guess so," Arnie said.

"No more fighting," Coach Green said. "I'm not kidding. I'll bench you both."

"We're cool," Arnie assured him.

Coach nodded and walked down the hall.

When the coach was gone, Norval asked, "*Are* we cool?"

"No. We're not," Arnie snapped. "But I'll make you a deal. Stay out of my way, and I'll stay out of yours."

"Suit yourself," Norval said. He didn't need to put up with any of Arnie's crazy mood swings. They had had been friends since grade school, and he hated to see their friendship end. But if that was how Arnie wanted it, there was nothing he could do.

———

Later, in the locker room, Coach Green approached Norval again. "What do you think? Is he all right to play?"

Norval came back at him, almost shouting. "Don't lay that on me—I can't make that call! I don't care what he does."

"I didn't ask you to make the call. I'll do that. I just asked for your opinion," the coach said. "I'm asking you what you think."

"I think he's all right," Norval said. Angry as he was, he wasn't going to be responsible for wrecking Arnie's dreams. "He's just nervous about getting a scholarship offer these days."

"And about his girlfriend?"

"Yeah, and that. But he's got it all wrong about me and her."

Coach Green stared at him for a long moment. "You're sure that's all it is? You're his friend. You know him better than I do."

"I think so. Pretty sure. Yeah."

Norval would never rat anyone out. That's not how he operated.

"Okay, then," Coach Green said. "Thanks for your input. The rest is up to me."

CHAPTER 17

As play-offs began, the Titans found themselves once again playing the Hempstead Huskers. Kadeem addressed the team in the locker room before everyone headed out to the field.

"Arnie, Norval. I've heard rumors that they're going to come after you two hard. Arnie, you keep running interference for Norval. But I want the rest of you guys watching Arnie. Look alert. I don't want him getting creamed out there. He's one of our fastest guys, and we need him."

Arnie smiled as Kadeem recognized his speed.

Norval was sure that he and Kadeem shared the same concerns about Arnie. "Have you spoken to Coach?" he asked as they prepared to leave the locker room.

"Not yet," Kadeem admitted. "Somehow I just can't bring myself to do it."

"Me neither," Norval said.

"We'll try to cover him as best we can, keep him from getting hit," Kadeem said. "Want to make an agreement? If he goes down again this game, we talk to the coach afterward. Okay?"

Norval was glad at the suggestion. Lying to the coach was starting to bother him. There were only a few more games left in the season. If they could cover Arnie, keep him from getting hit, then he'd have the time to recover. If that was impossible, they'd have him sidelined. Even if talking to Coach didn't feel right, they'd have to do it.

"Definitely," Norval agreed. "That's what

we have to do."

The Huskers tackled Arnie again and again during the first two quarters. More than once, Norval and Kadeem exchanged worried glances. If the Huskers were serious about targeting Arnie, there was no way to completely protect him.

Arnie wasn't making it easy for them, either. He fumbled the ball twice, and he wasn't running at his usual speed. He was off his game, even though his teammates were doing their best to pick up the slack.

Coach Green called a time-out. "Johnson, I want you to sit out," he said.

Arnie threw his arms wide, and Norval waited for the explosion.

"I can play, Coach," Arnie said calmly. "There's nothing wrong with me. Seriously."

Coach Green squinted, scrutinizing Arnie. His expression seemed to soften. "Sit out for a while. I'll decide if I'm going to put you in later."

Kadeem and Norval looked to each other with relief. Coach Green had made the call, and it was the right one.

The game was tight as halftime approached,

with the Titans trailing the Huskers by a few points. Coach Green pulled Arnie's replacement out of the game. "Get in there, Johnson," he said.

"Yes, sir, Coach," Arnie said, putting his helmet on. "You won't regret it."

When play resumed, Kadeem passed the ball to Norval, who zigzagged his way down the field. Arnie flanked him as the Southside fans cheered wildly.

A Husker defender appeared at Norval's side. Then three defensive players ran into view nearby. Jerome dashed between them and Norval. The Hempstead players flanked Jerome on both sides, then passed him, heading for Norval. Norval saw an open player in a Southside jersey—Arnie. He grimaced and lateralled him the football.

Arnie snagged the ball over the head of a defender.

Instantly the Husker defense crossed the field toward Arnie. Two more defenders appeared to Arnie's right. The five of them brought Arnie down at the thirty-yard line and piled on as the ref blew his whistle.

Norval remembered Coach's words from earlier: *If one player runs into another player at full speed, that's the same as getting hit by a car going forty miles an hour.* Was this equal to five cars?

The Hempstead players got up and headed back toward their teammates. Norval waited for Arnie to rise—and he did. Slowly. But rather than joining the other Titans, he just stood there.

Norval ran up to Arnie. "Are you okay?"

Arnie didn't seem to even hear him.

"Arnie!"

Still Arnie didn't respond.

"Can you see me?" Norval asked him.

Another whistle blasted. The coaches had called time-out. Coach Green and Coach Gannon were crossing the field toward them.

"You're . . . jumping," Arnie murmured. "Everything is jumping." He bent forward and vomited through his facemask.

"Come on," Coach Green said with calm firmness, and he put his arm around Arnie's shoulders. "Let's get you to the bench. "

This time Arnie didn't argue. He let Coach Green steer him off the field.

CHAPTER 18

Norval watched as Arnie sat on the bench and the medics looked him over. A burly young medic named Phil shined a small flashlight in Arnie's eyes.

"One pupil is more dilated than the other," Phil reported to another medic. He then held up one finger. "Try to follow my finger with your eye," Phil said, and he slowly drew a straight line in the air in front of Arnie.

Phil looked his partner and shook his head.

"He's not following."

Next Phil held out two fingers to Arnie. "Grab my fingers as hard as you can," he said.

Arnie did as he was told.

Again, Phil shook his head. "Weak grip," he reported to the other medic. "Can you describe to me how you're feeling, Arnie?" Phil asked.

"Sick," Arnie answered. "And I'm seeing things weird. One minute everything is blurred. Then it's jumpy and flickering. Sometimes I see two of things."

"Probable traumatic occipital lobe injury. Possibly secondary impact syndrome," Phil said to the other medic. "Let's bring the ambulance around. Arnie, we're taking you the hospital, okay? They'll need to run some tests on you."

"What kind of tests?" Norval asked.

"A CAT scan and probably an MRI. They'll want to get a look at his brain."

"Are your parents in the stands, Arnie?" Coach Green asked.

Arnie didn't reply.

"They don't usually come to the games," Norval told him.

"Okay. I'll call them," Coach Green said.

The medics left for a moment. Norval heard the whoop of an ambulance siren as they brought the vehicle to the edge of the field. Then they unloaded a stretcher and strapped Arnie onto it.

"Can I go with him?" Norval asked.

"Are you family?" Phil asked. Norval shook his head. "Then you can't. Sorry."

"You have a game to finish, Norval," Coach Green said. "Coach Gannon will follow them to the hospital. He'll stay until Arnie's parents arrive."

The other players and the cheerleaders gathered as the medics carried Arnie toward the ambulance. "Will he be all right?" Lara asked Norval.

"I don't know," Norval said. "I hope so."

CHAPTER 19

N orval's feet crossed the goal line, and
the crowd went wild. He'd scored the
winning touchdown. The Titans were headed
to the semifinals!

Despite the crowd's cheers, Norval found it
hard to feel happy. He blamed himself for not
speaking to Coach Green sooner. Arnie was
in the hospital, and he could have prevented
it. Once Coach Green had told Norval what
to look for, he'd known almost right away that

Arnie was dealing with a concussion.

He noticed that Kadeem wasn't looking too thrilled either, even as their teammates jumped and shouted with joy.

"I feel for the guy," Kadeem said as the crowd started to scatter. "I'm pretty sure I've had a concussion or two. I've had some of those symptoms. But they always go away."

"Your brain probably had time to heal," Norval said.

"Maybe. It was just luck if that's the case. I knew those Miller scouts were watching Arnie. I didn't want to mess up his chances. Since I've always ended up all right, I hoped Arnie would too. It's not fair. Why did I get better, and Arnie just kept getting worse?"

"It could be your position," Norval said. "The quarterback doesn't get hit as much. Your brain has had time to heal between hits. And Arnie always ran good interference for me."

Kadeem scowled. "Man, I want to play pro ball, but even that's not worth having my brain scrambled. If I have to sit out the season and let my brain heal, then that's what I have to do, even if it means losing my scholarship. That would suck, though."

"I know," Norval agreed.

Kadeem shook his head. "We should have said something. But we didn't."

Coach Green approached them from the sidelines. "I hope you boys are happy now," he said.

"Us?" Norval shouted. He could no longer control himself. "We're not the guys in charge! You are. You're the one who made the call."

"Norval's right," Kadeem said. "It isn't right to put all that on us."

"Face it! You wanted the win, so you played Arnie. I hope you're happy!" Norval shouted.

Coach Green's face turned red with anger. "Watch your mouths, or you won't play for the rest of the season. I don't care how good you are." With that, he turned away.

Norval watched Coach Green go, cursing him under his breath. Then he and Kadeem headed to the locker room in silence.

Once inside, Norval called the hospital. He learned that Arnie was being kept overnight for observation. He could have visitors, though, from six to eight.

"Want to go see him?" Norval asked Kadeem.

"Let's go tomorrow and give the guy time to rest," Kadeem said.

Norval nodded. He got dressed and met up with his parents, who had come to see the game. "You're not going out with your friends?" his mother asked.

"I wouldn't have any fun," Norval told her.

CHAPTER 20

T he following afternoon Norval and
Kadeem went over to the hospital.
Maritza and Lara were leaving Arnie's room
when Norval and Kadeem arrived.

"How is he?" Norval asked.

"Pretty messed up," Maritza replied.

Arnie's parents and his doctor were at
Arnie's bedside, watching as Arnie drew on a
pad. Arnie looked up as Norval and Kadeem
came in, but he didn't acknowledge them. It

was almost as if he didn't know who they were.

Glancing at Arnie's paper, Norval saw that Arnie was drawing clock faces. At least, Norval guessed that they were supposed to be clocks. The one Arnie was working on had the squiggly, irregular shape of an amoeba. Some of the numbers floated inside the clock face. Others were completely outside of it. He had forgotten to draw in the hands of the clock entirely.

The doctor, a petite, dark-haired woman, took the paper from Arnie and showed Arnie's parents. "We'll need to run more neurological tests," she said quietly. "The MRI later today will give us a better sense of what areas of the brain have been injured."

"How do we fix this?" Arnie's father asked. His brow was creased with worry. "Lots of rest and rehabilitation," the doctor said. "I suggest keeping him in a rehabilitation center until he stabilizes. Then he can get help as an outpatient."

"What kind of help?" Arnie's mother asked.

"He'll work with a physiatrist, someone trained in brain injury recovery. There are exercises that can help the brain recover function after a trauma. The brain can rewire itself. He'll need to be where his brain has the ideal conditions to do so."

Norval jumped into the conversation. "Will he recover completely?"

"We don't really know," the doctor replied. "He's young. Young people have a remarkable ability to recover. On the other hand, his youth makes him even more vulnerable when it comes to concussion."

"Why is that?" Norval asked.

The doctor asked Arnie's parents if they minded Kadeem and Norval being there before she answered any further questions. Arnie's parents said they didn't—the boys were Arnie's friends.

"High school athletes suffer more from the damage of concussion than even college athletes," the doctor said. "Because high school players are still young, their skulls are thinner. Their nervous systems are not fully developed. High school students are also less likely to know the symptoms of a concussion."

"How bad is Arnie's concussion?" Kadeem asked.

"Arnie has a severe, grade-three concussion," the doctor reported. "I imagine that this isn't his first. After a first concussion, second and third concussions are more likely. This young man should not have been playing football."

"Will he miss a lot of school?" Norval asked.

"He's looking at six to eight months of rehabilitation. We don't want him working too hard on his schoolwork during that time because his brain needs to rest."

This was bad news. Arnie would not graduate with the rest of them. He looked at Arnie to see how he was taking it.

Arnie just stared blankly. Norval wondered if he even understood what was being said.

Mrs. Johnson approached her son. "Arnie, your friends have come to see you. Aren't you going to say hello?"

"Hey, buddy," Kadeem said. "You feeling any better?"

"Hey, Arnie. It's me," Norval added. "How are you?"

Arnie didn't respond.

"He needs to rest," the doctor told Norval and Kadeem. "You'd better go."

"He's going to be better, though, right?" Norval asked.

"I hope so," the doctor answered. "But it's going to take time."

Kadeem and Norval said good-bye and left the room. They walked down the hospital corridor without talking. "This sucks," Kadeem said, wiping wetness from his eyes.

All Norval could say was, "Sure does."

CHAPTER 21

Norval made an effort to see Arnie at the rehabilitation center at least twice a week. Other teammates went too. It got harder in the last weeks of football season, when Coach Green started keeping the team after practice to go over new plays or to watch footage of other teams in the play-offs. But Norval didn't stop.

Around the time the season ended, Arnie seemed to recognize Norval again, but he was hostile—friendly one minute and then nasty the next.

Norval tried to be understanding, but it wasn't easy. He tried to remember that this was his friend, that Arnie's brain injury was making him so moody.

In early December, Arnie entered rehab. One afternoon in January, Norval came to sit with him in the rehab center's lounge.

He wanted to talk about all the offers their teammates had received, but he knew the subject wasn't guaranteed to boost Arnie's mood. So he told him about the winter dance that had just taken place. The gym had been decorated as an ice pond. Sadie had looked beautiful in a silver spangled dress.

"Norval, would you do me a favor?" Arnie said when Norval was finished. "Don't come here anymore. Okay?"

"Why?" Norval asked.

"It's just . . . it's not fair that this happened to me. Seeing you all healthy and going off to winter dances, while I have to sit here—"

"Aw, come on, Arnie. That doesn't make

sense. I have to talk about something. You never even liked those dances."

"I don't care if it makes sense. My brain doesn't work anymore. Don't you get that? I'm not supposed to make sense. Besides, you must have better things to do. Why do you care what happens to me?"

"I'm your friend," Norval said.

"If you were my friend, you would have said something when you saw me acting weird."

"I did!" Norval replied. "You wouldn't listen to me. You begged me not to tell the coach."

"If you were really my friend, you would have done something," Arnie said.

Arnie's words hit Norval hard. Arnie was blaming him for all the things he was blaming himself for.

"Now get out of here!" Arnie shouted. "Go off to prom and graduation. I don't care. I can't stand the sight of your face. I don't need your pity! Get lost."

Norval looked around, flustered. Other people in the room were watching. They could hear everything Arnie was saying.

"I'm not kidding! Go!" Arnie shouted.

Norval felt like Arnie had punched him. His face burned with shame. As he rushed out of the room, one of therapists, a man in his thirties, caught Norval by the arm.

"I heard what happened," the therapist said. "Try not to let it get to you. Rage and depression are two of the side effects he's dealing with."

"But the things he's saying are true," Norval replied.

"Are you the only one to blame?" the therapist asked. "From what he said, it sounded to me like you tried to get through to him."

"I did," Norval said, feeling tears building behind his eyes. "I didn't do enough, though."

"I'm sure you did what you could," the therapist said. "Arnie has to get through this on his own now."

CHAPTER 22

N orval knocked on the door of Sadie's
apartment. Her mother let him in. When
Sadie stepped into the living room, he gasped.
Her hair was curled and pinned up on her
head, and her emerald green strapless prom
gown swirled around her curves. "Wow!" he
whispered.

"You look pretty nice too," she said with a
smile. "You should wear a tux all the time."

He grinned.

"I can't believe graduation is next week," Sadie's mom said. "I am so proud of you two. To think that a few months from now you'll both be off to college."

Norval smiled at Sadie. She'd been awarded an athletic scholarship to cheer at Wendell College. He'd received an offer from Miller College. They'd miss each other, but neither college was so far from home that they couldn't come home to see each other on some weekends.

Sadie's cell buzzed. "Hi, Lara," she said, answering it, then covered the phone to talk to her mother. "Could we pick up Lara on the way to the school?" she asked. "Her date's car broke down."

"Who is she going with?" Norval asked.

Sadie rolled her eyes. "Jerome."

The mention of Lara brought Norval back to Arnie. He hadn't been back to school, wasn't going to graduate with them, and wouldn't be at prom.

"You're thinking of Arnie, aren't you?" Sadie asked.

"How did you know?" Norval asked.

"You always get that faraway look in your eyes when something reminds you of him."

"Maybe I should go see him again. Even if he doesn't want me there."

"Come on, you two," Sadie's mother urged them, car keys in her hand. "We'd better get going if we have to pick up your friends."

Sadie put her hand on Norval's arm and smiled at him. "Just have fun tonight. You can decide what to do about Arnie later."

Norval spent the summer after graduation working at a day camp. Near the summer's end, as he watched the last of his campers leave the park with their parents, he saw someone heading toward him. The young man had an unsteady gait. Norval didn't recognize him at first. And then suddenly he did.

It was Arnie.

"Hey, man," Arnie greeted him. "They told me you were working here." For the first time in months, a smile lit Arnie's face.

Norval drew Arnie into a warm embrace. "Arnie! How've you been?"

"Okay. Much better. Sorry for being such a jerk last time I saw you."

"Don't worry about it." Norval was so happy to see his friend that he couldn't hold a grudge. "Sorry I didn't come to see you after that. I thought about it, but I worried it'd just upset you."

"It probably would have. I was going through some rough times back then. I treated a lot of people badly."

"You were dealing with some hard stuff," Norval said. "How's your head now?"

Arnie smiled. "Still healing, I guess. It takes me forever to read a book or take a test. I'm going back to school in the fall, but I'll have to get extra time to do my assignments. I have a whole specialized education program that's been worked out for me, though. So it should be all right. With any luck, I can get into Southside Community College. Football is completely out. That goes without saying."

"You'll find something else," Norval said.

"Hah. Yeah. I'm Bouncing Arnie Johnson, aren't I?"

Norval slapped him on the back and grinned. "You are, man. That's the truth for sure."

"Can I buy you a slice somewhere?" Arnie offered.

"Absolutely," Norval said. "Let's go."

About the Author

Suzanne Weyn has written many books for children and young adults. For a complete list, go to suzanneweynbooks.com. She holds a Masters degree in teaching adolescents and has taught writing at New York University and City College of New York.

SOUTHSIDE HIGH

ARE YOU A SURVIVOR?

check out all the books in the

SURVIVING SOUTH SIDE

collection